The Coat

George Zito

Published in 2019 by FeedARead.com Publishing

Copyright © George Zito. 2019.

The author or authors assert their moral right under the Copyright, Designs and Patents Act, 1988, to be identified as the author or authors of this work.

A CIP catalogue record for this title is available from the British Library.

The Coat

A big thank you to Sarah from the Interlude Café. Thank you for your amazing food, beverages and for letting me use The Interlude Café in my story.

A big thank you to Inspired Neighbourhood CIC who do amazing community work in Bradford.

All money raised will go to help Bradford's Primary and Secondary Schools Mental Health Champions.

Contents

Behaviour Cafe

The tube train stops briefly in the dark tunnel
and slowly makes its way through to the light.
It rocks the packed commuters side to side.
Moving from the dark unsecure to the light of
hope.

Like life the train's journey takes you down a
track. Sometimes there are dark tunnels, in
which you move into the light. The journey can
be full of obstacles and chaos. During the dark
times or chaos, the train will need help to get
back on the right track.

Rhythmically like a heart beat the train beats on
the tracks through the underground stations of
London.

It stops at Southfields underground station. A well-dressed man stands from his seat, ready to exit onto the platform. His clothes are well tailored and dated. His overcoat is a heavy camel wool overcoat, navy blue in colour. He is wearing a double breasted navy pinstripe suit, with turned up trousers, a buttoned down collar shirt and gold cufflinks with the initials G.C engraved. He is carrying a dark brown Fedora felt trilby hat. The hat has a black ribbon band around. His shoes were Oxford black and white brogues.

The man waited for the doors to open and moved with the busy crowd of travellers.

He looked at the sign on the platform, it read Southfields Station.

On the platform he saw a coffee shop and noticed they were selling newspapers. He walked over and looked at the newspaper. It was the first of December 2020. He exited the tube station via the concrete stairs and put on his trilby hat. He tilted the trilby to the left side of his head.

The rain poured down on a cold winter's day. He made his way walking, down Wimbledon Park Road and then onto Merton Road. He walked with a swagger in his step, looking in amazement at the people, shops and cars.

He was heading towards The Park Tavern Pub on Merton Road. The rain poured down and he kept his head slightly down, as not to get rain on his face.

A roughly shaven man then bumped into the well-dressed man.

"Got the time mate?"

The man stopped and with a friendly smile looked at his watch. When he looked up to give the time, the unshaven man had a knife in his hand. A knife similar to a Commando dagger.

"Give me your money and phone now!"

The man calmly focused on the man with the knife. He felt totally calm, but could see how agitated and threatening this man was.

"I have not got any money or a phone on me. But you can take my expensive coat, it is worth a lot of money."

"Quick then, gimme the coat now!" The unshaven man said desperately.

The well-dressed man took off his navy blue coat and passed it to the man with the knife. The mugger was surprised how heavy the coat was, he grabbed it and ran off down Merton Road.

The rain continued to downpour.

The well-dressed man stood shocked in the rain and blustery weather. He kept his cool and calmly walked on. No one stopped in the street, to see if he was okay. The man was cold, lonely and shocked. He decided to walk back to the train station.

The Unshaven Man

The unshaven man who had robbed the coat was Tom Jackson. Tom was homeless and now on heroin. He ran with the coat down Merton Road into King George's Park. In the park, he slowed down and put the heavy wool coat on. Then started to go through the pockets.

He was feeling odd, weird and emotional, a real sense of love and warmth. This feeling was odd, even spiritual. Something had taken a hold of him, something deeply spiritual. For the first time in a year he could make sense of his feelings again. He became overwhelmed with love and guilt. He fell to his knees on the wet, muddy grass of the football pitch.

He looked towards the sky as the rain poured onto Tom's face. Tears flowed with sorrow and anger. His journey of life had taken him to a dark place.

"What sort of animal have I become? A low life scum bag, who mugs someone for this stupid coat. God help me, why I am doing this? To feed my bloody addiction. I am weak and useless."

The coat felt alive, magical and supportive. Tom felt a sense of love and care for him. These were feelings of Tom from the past. The coat not only kept him dry, but as he felt inside the coat, there were many intricate pockets.

The first pocket he came to, had some food in it. He wolfed his favourite sandwich down, bacon, lettuce and tomato. As he got up off his knees, there were two people walking past. They casted Tom a glance and then they looked away. The people were intent on walking past Tom as quick as they could. He saw them avoiding him.

"Oi! Look at you judging me, you don't know nothing about me. I was a bloody Royal Marines Officer a few years back and would have kicked your arses. Sticking your bleeding noses up at me."

Tom was now living off the streets of London and heroin had become his companion.

The onlookers looked away, avoiding any eye contact.

Tom reached inside the coat, there was another deep pocket. Inside there were some train tickets, with his name on. The destination of the tickets, read Shipley, West Yorkshire. There was also some money alongside the tickets, a hundred pounds. The train journey was arranged for the next day.

In another pocket there was a hotel reservation receipt, booked in his name. It was for a hotel near to Kings Cross train station.

But the thought of one hundred pounds and how much heroin he could buy, became his focus. He kept feeling the money and the train tickets.

Tom thought he was hallucinating, "This can't be real, money and these tickets. I just need to get some gear to settle me down."

He decided to walk in the direction of a local dealer in the pouring rain and blustering wind. But the weight of the coat had some magnetic pull on Tom. For some reason, he was being controlled and it became an impossible task to go in the direction of the dealer. Every step was like he was wearing a weighted diving suit and diving bell helmet.

He found himself directed by a powerful force or energy in the direction of Southfields Tube Station. He tried to resist but the force was too great.

He caught the tube and the strong pull of the coat made him get off at Earls Court station and then the train to King's Cross station.

He exited Kings Cross tube station and felt controlled by the coat. The coat was so over powering. Tom found himself in a back street, at the Halfway Hotel. He entered the reception and was greeted by a woman with a kind smile.

"You must be Mr. Jackson."

"Yes, how did you know?"

She just smiled and gave Tom his electronic room key card. "Your room number is ten. Included in the price is dinner and breakfast. There was a note to say you will be catching the nine am train to Shipley West Yorkshire."

"I don't understand who has paid for my stay and train ticket?"

"Don't worry Mr. Jackson everything has been taken care for."

"By who?"

"By you Mr. Jackson."

Tom was tired and desperate for a fix, he was feeling agitated, sweaty and extremely warm under the coat. He headed for room ten.

Tom tried to loosen the coat, but the coat was too powerful. He could not remove it. He became really frustrated. The coat felt so reassuring and had a calming influence. He tried to relax by turning the TV on to distract him. He turned the TV on and started to flick through the channels, on every channel he could see his former self. He decided to sit down and watch. He could see himself as a former Royal Marines Commando officer. Then a Narrator started to speak like a documentary programme.

"The last tour of Afghanistan for Captain Tom Jackson.

He was serving with 45 Commando. In camp
Bastion, Tom and his Sergeant Charlie
Ainsworth briefed their men on their final
mission."

"Both Tom and Charlie were battle hardy
veterans. After the briefing Tom and Charlie
motivated their troops."

On the TV, Tom told his men "All of you are
part of my family. We are with you all the
way. I have been so proud to be part of 45
Commando. I just want you all to be as safe as
possible out there. Keep being switched on,
thank you."

Charlie took over. "Right, listen in.

We are going to have some scran, then check our weapons and kit. We will be embarking at 0300 hours from Helman's Province to Shin Kalay. Right let's get some scran."

The Narrator carried on," Captain and the Sergeant sat with their men and they all ate together. There was a lot of banter and the men's spirits were high. Tom asked Charlie to come outside the mess."

"Charlie I just wanted to tell you how proud I am to have such a brave, brilliant sergeant and a really good friend."

Charlie shook hands with Tom. "We will get through this chaotic mess, with our arses intact."

The Narrator continued "Tom and Charlie got the patrol together."

Tom stood to and thanked every single person. "This mission is going to be a tough one! Let's use our experience to help the new members of the team and stick together through this adversity, making sure we come back safe. Let's be careful out there!"

The patrol boarded the Chinook helicopter. It was three AM, the sky was still and calm. The propellers were continually rotating, as the armed patrol boarded. Some of the patrol sat in silence just focusing on the task at hand. There was a lot of nervous energy and fidgeting.

The Chinook lowered over their drop zone and they quickly evacuated the helicopter and took cover. They had been dropped near to Shin Kalay. Tom led the patrol around the edge of a field, which was full of poppies in the long dense grass. The patrol moved slowly. The sun rose in the east. A spectacular orangey red, the haze of the bright sun glared across the valley.

The patrol moved slowly, as the heat of the sun intensified on them. The men wore protective armour and carried huge Bergen ruck sacks, their weapons and ammunition.

The men dripped in sweat, as these young men from all over the United Kingdom, moved through this difficult foreign terrain.

This patrol had been together for the entire tour of Afghanistan. These young men had witnessed previously the horrors of war, like the Intelligent Electronic Devices (IED's) which wounded colleagues loosing limbs and their friends dying. These men were haunted by their experiences.

The heat intensified which slowed the patrol. The patrol was halted by Tom. The patrol provided all round cover, while everyone took some fluids in. Tom advised they were nearing Shin Kalay, where they would be meeting their Afghanistan Army guides. The patrol comradery was high and the men were up for their challenge.

They were now coming out of cover and patrolling in open land. There seemed an eerie silence as they heard the noise of something evil. One of the Marines in the patrol heard a click. Then in slow motion an explosion blasted loudly, black smoke, deathly screams and rivers of blood. Tom and Charlie ran over to where eighteen year old Private Matthew Simmons laid. He shivered with trauma, his legs blown to pieces. Tom called for the medic and Charlie phoned for air casualty evacuation. Tom and the medic worked hard at getting an intravenous fluids in to the injured marine's veins, under severe shock. They gave morphine. The medic reduced the river of blood coming from the femoral arteries, where his legs should have been and applied two femoral tourniquets.

Then the patrol came under heavy gun fire and mortar rounds.

Tom got his signalmen to radio in airstrikes and passed on the coordinates. Within minutes jets flew over bombing the targets below. The whole patrol were involved in the firefight. The next thing a young woman was pushed out into a cornfield into the battle area. Bullets were now flying all over. Without thinking Tom shouted cover me, he ran and saved the woman. He had been wounded in his left arm and the next thing he and Private Simmons were at Camp Bastian.

After the forces, Tom had managed to get a flat in Merton Road, Wandsworth, London. He used his H.M. Forces medical discharge fund to train as a chef. He was now qualified and was in the process of living his dream. To get his own restaurant.

He was coming out of Covent Garden Tube Station, when he noticed a homeless man selling the Big Issue.

The man looked familiar and Tom was drawn to the man. As he got close he realised it was his Sergeant Charlie.

"Charlie, it's me mate. Tom"

Charlie looked embarrassed and did not know what to say.

"What's happened Charlie?

"I had trouble settling back into Civvy Street. I just couldn't cope, just started getting flashbacks. I became a recluse and lost my house."

Tom put his hand on Charlie's shoulder.

"Listen mate, my flat has an extra room. I want you to have it, until you get sorted."

"You don't want me making a mess of your life."

Tom smiled "It's an order sergeant."

Charlie was a proud man, but was in a dark place.

He shook Tom's hand. "You are a life saver. You don't want me making a mess of your life."

Tom smiled "It's an order sergeant."

Charlie was a proud man, he shook Tom's hand. "You are a life saver."

The Narrator continued "Charlie moved in with Tom. He needed a right hand man to help him through this business adventure, someone loyal. Tom payed for Charlie to train as a chef, over the next year. Charlie was so thankful.

Tom's new restaurant was in Southfields, London. It was a perfect place, across the road from Southfields Tube Station. Tom and Charlie wanted this restaurant to be different and make a difference to people's lives.

They decided to employ staff who have had mental health issues. They both felt strongly about this and wanted to give people a chance to get back into work. They called the restaurant "Behaviour Café."

Over the weeks, word had spread about the quality of the food. They became so busy, that they had to start bookings for tables.

Food critics got wind of this bizarre but brilliant eatery. They were not disappointed. Great reviews hit the press and food magazines.

The café went from strength to strength. The staff were inspired by Tom.

He really got them motivated and treated them all with great respect. He was like a father figure to all his staff.

Tom told Charlie he needed to speak to him, when they both got home that night. He decided to open up to Charlie, he had been struggling to come to terms with his sexuality.

"I am gay Charlie."

Charlie hugged him and said "Me too. I have been struggling with how people are going to judge me. Commandos should be real men, right."

"You are so right, the difficult thing is Charlie, I have fallen in love with you." They both kissed and hugged.

The Narrator continued, "Tom used to finish at three pm to have a break and would leave Charlie in charge. This was becoming a daily habit. Charlie was concerned as he knew something was not right with Tom.

Tom at work was the boss, everyone saw him as a role model, but inside he felt detached from reality. Charlie had noticed that his partner was not his normal self.

Tom decided to leave on this day at lunchtime and left Charlie in charge. The café was so busy, Charlie did not have time to think about the boss. He worked busily into the evening. But Tom did not return to work. On the TV it showed himself going to a dealer to buy heroin.

Charlie was really concerned about Tom and tried to phone and text him. There was no reply.

Tom was in a dark place and traumatised by what happened in Afghanistan. He could not cope and was not in control and took to the streets. He was suffering from Post-Traumatic Stress Disorder. He felt isolated and suffering internally. Charlie and his staff always saw Tom as the strong one, the leader. But Tom on the inside was hurting and desperate. Heroin became his crutch and friend. It was in this darkness that Tom started his homeless journey. The TV showed Charlie and how his heart was broken and he felt immense guilt.

The narrator pointed to Tom. "You need no longer suffer alone and a greater power has taken responsibility for your dark times. Take the light and be proud of who you are. Let go of the guilt, shame and realise that war puts you in unhuman situations, where choice is not on your side."

There was a bright white light beaming from the TV, all around Tom.

Interlude Café

The next thing Tom was on a train to Shipley, West Yorkshire. He sat on a seat near to the window. He felt peaceful, like the storm in his head had calmed and the sea was gentle and calm.

When he arrived at Shipley Train Station, he asked a man in the station café for directions to the Interlude Café. When he entered the Interlude café, a lady with a large smile welcomed him in. She was wearing nineteen forties clothes, an apron and a hair net. The café was all done out like during the Second World War.

Glen Miller music played in the background.

The lady came over and brought a pot of tea

and some hand- made scones.

Tom smiled "Thank you, but I have not

ordered?"

"It's on the house, you look like you need it a

good cuppa." The lady left him and went down

some stairs.

A man with a trilby hat entered the café. Tom

did not recognise him. He approached Tom.

The man tilted his trilby back, "Relax Tom,

everything is going to be okay. I know now

why you took my coat. I also know about your

partner Charlie.

He really loves you and misses you deeply.

Also all your staff at Behaviour Café miss you.

Since getting to this café, what have you

learnt?"

Tom drank a slurp of tea and then let out all his

trapped emotions and began to cry. I was

strong for everyone else, but I felt I couldn't

ask for help. I suppose I thought asking for

help was a weakness."

"What if we could give you another chance to

go back to the life you deserve? If you have

love and support in your life, you can heal and

be you again. You have seen inhuman things

and you had the responsibility of getting your

men back alive.

Could you pass my coat back?"

"What's going on, I don't understand?"

"It is Christmas Eve, in a while you will be transported outside the Behaviour Café. The snow is falling there, Charlie has been working hard to keep this restaurant open. He is suffering. Go in and let the power of love take over. Love of Charlie, love from your staff, customers and your love of food."

The well-dressed man put the coat on and raised his hat to the lady in the café. Ciao."

The well-dressed man and Tom vanished from the café and appeared outside the Behaviour Café. It was snowing, the man shook Tom's hand. Tom entered the café.

Green Door on the Wall

It's nineteen seventy six, the sun was shining brightly on Wandsworth, London. It's been a difficult time for Margaret Croft, since her husband gambled the family home and left. She is now renting a room in Balvernie Grove Wandsworth, with her two sons. Steven was six and James was four years of age. Margaret Croft was late for her cleaning job. As she scurries around, the children played and laughed. She grabbed their shoes and rushed to put them on. She finally closed the door to her upstairs flat. She hurried up the road with each son in her hands. She walked so fast, the boys were struggling to keep up.

She marched up to Merton Road, and stood at

the bus stop opposite the Park Tavern pub.

Steven saw a shining coin in the road, it was ten

pence. Steven put all his focus on the shining

coin. He walked in front of his mum and

stepped off the curb, to grab the coin.

Everything then went into slow motion. Steven

felt an arm pull him back, as he was pushed

back to the curb.

James looked in horror, as he heard the

screeching of brakes. His mum was hit by an

oncoming car. She was thrown into the road,

where she laid lifeless.

Her two traumatised boys became hysterical with tears, as they tried to wake their mum up. She laid pooling with blood and silent.

There was an Italian bakery close by, the bakers came out and moved the boys inside. They did their best to calm and reassure the boys. But the boys were hysterical and could not hold back their tears.

The ambulance and the police arrived. A policeman came into the bakers, he took his hat off and felt so sad for these two boys. He knew how bad this was and the outcome for these kids was not a good one. It was only when he spoke to one of the bakers, that he found out the boys had witnessed their own mum getting hit.

This tragic news was one of the difficulties of the job, especially when it involves kids and young people.

Local witnesses were full of tears, as they entered the bakers to offer support to these little boys.

The policeman called a car, as he had to take the boys to Wandsworth Police Station.

Wandsworth Police Station

At the police station they were met by a female Police Officer and a Social Worker. Later that day, the tragic news of the boy's mother came through to the police station. Their mother Margaret had died of her injuries. The Police Officer broke the sad news to the boys, she could not hold back the tears and hugged both boys. They were distraught and crying for their mum.

Steven and James got in a car with the social worker and the police officer. They looked so lost, how could these children understand. They spent the remaining years in foster care, with different families.

As Adults

Steven at the age of eighteen decided to join the army in 1988. He flourished in the army and progressed through the ranks and gained selection to the SAS. He was now involved in frontline operations in Afghanistan.

James got a job in a bank when he left school, it was here that he met his love of his life Joanne. When he got to the age of thirty two he decided to join the police force. They both got married just before he joined the police.

Police Passing Out Parade

It was a hot summers day, James was busy preparing his police uniform for this special day.

He could not wait to show Joanne, who was now pregnant, how proud he was for passing the police training. Also his brother Steven had managed to get leave, to attend his brother's special day.

It was a perfect day. The Police band played, as the recruits marched behind. After the marching, the Chief Inspector did his speech and presented awards.

He announced the best recruit "this person has given a hundred percent in all areas of his work. The best recruit goes to James Croft."

James won best recruit and proudly marched up to get his award.

After the ceremony James went over to see his wife and brother. James kissed his wife and hugged his brother Steven. Steven patted James on the back, "Look at you, best recruit."

James smiled "Look at you Special Forces." Steven always played things down. "I'm so proud of you both. I have got you some presents in the car."

After the parade Steven helped James load all his police kit into his four by four vehicle.

Steven drove James and Joanne to their home.

Steven could only stay for two nights.

James's House

Steven helped James with all his bags and uniform. Then Steven went back to his car, he carried many bags of wrapped presents and gave them to Joanne. He did several more trips, in which he bought in a brand new cot. James and Joanne were overwhelmed. Joanne kissed Steven on the cheek. "You shouldn't have, this must have cost you a fortune?" Steven pulled out an envelope out from his coat. He gave it to Joanne. Joanne opened it, it was a beautiful baby card, with two smaller envelopes inside. She opened both envelopes. One had a five hundred pound voucher for Hamley's toyshop, in London.

The other envelope had a cheque for five thousand pounds.

Joanne had tears streaming down her face.

"We can't accept this, you will need this money."

Steven smiled, "Look in the forces, there is nothing to spend your money on. Also, I won't take no for an answer."

James put his arm around Steven, "I do not know what to say."

"That makes a change," Steven laughed.

Celebration

That night Steven took his family to an expensive restaurant. It was one of those restaurants run by a TV chef. It had Michelin star ratings. At their table the brothers laughed and cried, reflecting back to their childhood. It had been difficult for Steven, as he felt tremendous guilt over their Mums accident.

"If I wouldn't have gone for that bloody coin, Mum would be still alive."

James looked at Steven and reassured him. "It was not your fault. That fella was driving too fast."

Joanne held James's hand, as they eat their food.

They all finished the night with coffees. Steven settled the bill and asked for a taxi. When they got home, Steven seemed upset.

"What's up bruv?"

Steven put his arm around James. "I'm so proud of you both. I can't wait to see my nephew."

Joanne turned around to face Steven, "What makes you think you are going to get a nephew?"

Steven confidently said "I just know."

The next morning Steven cooked breakfast for his family. After breakfast James helped Steven with his bags and placed them in the boot of the car.

James gave Steven a big hug. "I'm always worried about you in Afghanistan. Why don't you call it a day and join the police force?"

Steven looked away, "I'll be alright James. You know I have always been one for adventure."

Joanne was very weepy. The baby was due in five weeks.

Wandsworth Police Station

James joined his new police station at Wandsworth. For the first month he was going to shadow an experienced officer. This would help him with the area and environment he would be dealing with.

After the first few days of induction and health and safety, his real life police training started. The experienced officer Nick Flower, had seen it all. He had been policing for twenty years, with the scars to show. Wandsworth was classed as a challenging area. It had proper gangsters who were armed and violent, drugs, vice, burglaries, muggings.

Day Two

They got their briefing from their Sergeant. He always finished his briefing sessions with "Be careful out there and don't do anything stupid."

Nick took James first to the Arndale Centre, off Merton Road. "Listen James, the Arndale centre is a hive of criminality. So keep your eyes peeled and don't say anything that might antagonise."

James calmly nodded "ok Nick."

Nick walked confidently and alert. As they entered the Arndale Centre, there was a young man stood outside Traders Hall, glue sniffing.

He was extremely anxious and agitated, especially when he saw the boys in blue. Nick left this one for James. James knew the young man "Hi ya Maurice, it's okay. It's James, how you doing?"

"James, James Croft. Is that you man?

"Yeah, Maurice, I'm just checking you are alright?"

"Yeah man, feeling good now. The plane has landed."

"Everything good at home Maurice?"

"No. It's been five years."

"I know your brother was killed by a rival gang."

"He was my young brother. Gary got a bullet in the head. He had nothing to do with gangs! He was walking his dog, when they drove by and shot him.

James put his arm around Maurice, "I'm so sorry mate."

Nick lost his patience, he pulled James's arm off Maurice and wanted to arrest him for glue sniffing.

James turned and faced Nick. "What are you playing at? Maurice needs help not an arrest!"

"Here we go, a know it all. You are going to tell me that with my experience, I don't understand the streets!"

Maurice broke free from Nick and pulled a gun from his coat. "My parents have lost one son. I am going to shoot anyone who gets in my way."

James moved closer to Maurice, "come on Maurice, you are not a murderer. We will get them guys who shot your brother."

"I can't take it anymore. I don't want to live anymore."

A long awkward silence. Maurice had no expression on his face. "One shot, one shot, like the Deer Hunter. He pulled the trigger and Maurice fell to the ground, like a felled tree.

James moved forward and cleared the gun away from Maurice. James was holding Maurice on the floor. Blood pooled around them.

Nick radioed back to the station and called an ambulance.

James did his best to administer first aid, but Maurice was silent. The ambulance came and rushed him to the nearest hospital.

Nick was waiting for a patrol car to take them to the hospital. James got up with blood on his hands.

Nick looked angry, "you will need to get a blood test to rule out HIV." He coldly turned his back on James.

James's temper came out. "Is that all you can say. I had it under control, but your so called experience turned this situation into this. A man who was suffering and mentally ill. Christ, his brother was killed."

Nick just shrugged it off. "You are too attached. You won't last in the police, if you keep this up."

"How would you feel if someone had killed your brother and the murderer was still on the street? You try and explain that to Maurice's Mum."

"Listen Maurice had it coming. Glue sniffing and probably on drugs. He was a danger with a gun in his pocket. He was off his rocker."

"Believe it or not, Maurice was a good guy."

A patrol car pulled up and drove both of them to the hospital.

The Hospital

Maurice had died on arrival. Nick and James decided to make the call to Maurice's Mum, to break the bad news.

James knew Maurice and his family from school days. Maurice's Mum still lived in the same house. It was a terraced house with a red brick wall and a black gate.

James opened the rusty Iron Gate, which made a noise. He rang the bell on the wooden door. Both policemen took the helmets off. An elderly lady answered the door.

James looked upset. "Mrs. Jackson, I'm not sure if you remember me, James Croft? I would be grateful if my colleague and I could come inside."

"Why, what's happened?"

James sat Mrs. Jackson down. She said "I can't take any more bad news, I have already lost a son."

"I am very sorry Mrs. Jackson. I don't know how to break this bad news. Maurice took his own life today."

Mrs. Jackson froze and just stared into the air. Tears flowed down her worn face.

Nick rang for the family support officer to attend to Mrs. Jackson, while James comforted Maurice's Mum. When the Family Support Officer came, Nick pulled James away.

The Streets of Wandsworth

James went home after his first day. Nick commented "that this was no ordinary day, in this area of work anything can happen."

James got home after a fourteen hour day. Joanne had cooked their teas. He gave Joanne a big kiss and kissed her stomach. "Where's my little baby?"

Joanne put the plates on the table. "I can't wait till the baby comes now. I'm so restless and uncomfortable. How was your first day?"

I am shadowing an experienced officer for the first month. His name is Nick. It's been a challenging day, but this is what I joined up for."

James was looking forward to his next week with Nick. It was shift work and they were on earlies. He got to work for five am.

On their patrol, Nick was pointing out the trouble makers, gangsters, prostitutes, drug dealers.

The big problem at the moment was gangs. Nick pointed out a notorious gang leader called Psycho. He highlighted that this person will stop at nothing, to get his way.

Nick said "We think it was Psycho's gang who killed Maurice's brother. But we do not have the evidence.

People are scared to come forward and testify. Psycho's girlfriend has split with her so called lover and is now seeing another gang leader. In fact she has been seen with another gang leader called James Angel."

James listened intently. "It all seems like things are going to kick off."

"You see James, that fella Angel is not a bad lad. He has just got mixed in with the wrong crowd. His brother is Kiely Angel a DJ. He's a really nice lad. I hope his brother makes him see sense."

James and Nick walked past the Park Tavern
pub on Merton Road. Nick got a radio message
that a man had been attacked on Lainson Street.
Nick answered the call, "roger, on the way."
They both ran to Lainson Street, a few minutes
away. They could hear screams from some
maisonette flats. There was a lad on the floor
severely injured. He had been stabbed. He was
laying on his back, barely breathing.

James went to see if anyone had seen the
attacker. He wanted to know what direction he
went in, but nobody saw a thing.

Within minutes several patrol cars turned up, as
well as the ambulance and rapid response.

The ambulance crew were there now. The man on the floor had multiple stab wounds and was in a critical way.

The paramedics had set up intravenous fluids and arrested the bleeding. One of the medics said "We are off to St. George's Hospital."

Nick radioed for a patrol car to take them to the hospital. He was so angry and kicked the fence in the car park.

"Another young life, for what? Because he had a different baseball cap on, different to the other gang."

James reassured Nick, "We are just doing our best to protect people. Young people these days don't have no role models or family.

They feel gang life is their only way to be part of a family. This type of violence and behaviour is so sickening and pointless. Having a fight is one thing, this level of violence makes me feel sick in the pit of my stomach."

The Crime Investigation Team came and sealed the area off. A patrol car arrived and took Nick and James to the hospital. They arrived at the Accident and Emergency Department. The consultant in charge came over to Nick.

"Its bad news I am afraid. This poor young man has lost his life."

Nick took the news badly. He had seen this lad grow into a decent young man. He turned to James.

"What can we do to stop this violence?

The other day the government was saying that the crime figures were down. Do they really know what happens on the streets?

James nodded, "Without brave Policeman like you Nick, the world would be a far worse place. This is now a murder investigation."

They went back to Wandsworth Police station to write their report.

James went home after his shift to his beautiful wife. James had received a letter from his brother Steven.

It read "To my wonderful family, I hope everything is going well in the police force? I can't wait till my nephew arrives.

Going on operations won't be able to write for a while. Don't worry, love you all with all my heart."

The Call

While James was on day time duty, a call came in that a brawl between two rival gangs was kicking off, at the Arndale shopping Centre. James and his colleague took the call. They climbed in the police car and sped off with the siren blazing. James's adrenaline was flowing. He then got a call on his personal mobile, it was Joanne. Hi love, is everything alright?

Joanne was crying, "My waters have broken and I am going into labour."

James told his colleague. His colleague radioed in and advised that someone else needs to take the Arndale call. His colleague changed direction towards James's home.

James rang for an ambulance. Then phoned
Joanne, "honey take deep breaths, I am on my
way. I have called an ambulance, don't worry,
I am nearly home. Love you so much."

"Hurry James."

Within minutes James arrived at his home, his
colleague dropped him off.

"Don't worry I got this shout James. Let me
know when the baby is born."

James rushed to his house and tried to reassure
Joanne. Then the ambulance arrived. James
picked up the already packed bag with all
essential baby things.

The ambulance took them to the maternity unit
at St. George's hospital.

A midwife was allocated and twelve hours later their beautiful baby boy was born.

Both Joanne and James were delighted, James left a message on Steven's phone. He knew that he would not get the message straight away, as he was on active duty.

Joanne and James decided to name their son Steven. James was thrilled that Joanne agreed to call their son after his brave brother.

Back on Duty

James returned back on duty at Wandsworth Police Station. He had not heard anything from his brother for several months now. Although this was normal for Steven, James always worried for his brother.

All James's colleagues had chipped in some money to give him a card and a gift card for a hundred pounds.

The Inspector called everyone on duty into the operations room. He explained that a rival gang member's brother was shot in a drive by and now in a critical condition. The person was named as Joe Kielty.

The Inspector wanted to address the recent gang warfare and how they could prevent possible revenge attacks.

A Knock at the Door

Several days later Joanne was busy with her baby, when she heard a knock at the door.

There were two military policemen in uniform.

Joanne opened the door and quickly said "it's Steven!"

One of the Military Policemen confirmed demographics and asked if her husband James was in?

Joanne felt very anxious and rang James.

"James, you need to come home now, there are two military policemen here."

James got home. Joanne had tears streaming down her eyes.

James felt empty and everything seemed as if the world slowed down.

Both Military Policemen introduced themselves. The officer spoke quietly and told James that they had sad news that his brother had been killed in Afghanistan. He has been put forward for the Military Cross for bravery. James had all those feelings that he experienced when his mum died.

The Military Policeman continued to say "that Steven had saved a mother and her two children in a cross fire. The woman and her two sons survived. Your brother was a brave man and his colleagues have written this letter for you." He handed James the letter.

The other Military Policeman advised that there is a full Military Service for Steven next Friday at his residing barracks.

One of the Military Policeman put the kettle on and made James and Joanne a cup of tea.

James and Joanne held each other with such sadness. A sadness you can't understand unless you have lost someone you love. James could not stop the tears as they flowed down his face, landing like rain drops on to the beige lounge carpet.

Funeral

The church was packed with military people. Steven had the full military honours and a gun salute. During the funeral his colleagues told stories about Steven and described his years of bravery. But most of all Steven talked about his brother James and his sister in law and how he was soon to be a proud uncle.

After the funeral, James, Joanne and baby Steven drove home. James felt the loneliest person in the world. He could not believe he would never see his brother again.

When they got home, James looked at Joanne and said "hope you don't mind my love, but I need to get some fresh air."

Joanne cuddled her husband, "its fine I understand."

James walked to Wimbledon Park. It was a winters evening and he walked through the park, lost and heartbroken. At the lake he sat on a near-by bench that he and his brother Steven used to sit on. He remembered the great memories of pushing each other into the lake for fun. He felt in so much pain of losing his brother and wept uncontrollably.

Then from nowhere James was startled, as a well-dressed man with a trilby hat on and an expensive coat, sat next to him.

He looked at the stranger, he did not feel threatened.

The man did not look at me but he said "I am sorry for the loss of your brave brother."

"How did you know, are you a mate of his."

"Something like that."

James was shivering in the cold air and traumatised by his loss. The man gave him his blue wool tailored overcoat. "This coat is a special coat and will keep you warm."

James was in shock and put the coat over his shoulders and put his hands in the pockets. There he found the envelope that Steven had written, it had the voucher for Hamley's toy shop.

"I can't understand it, how could this envelope end up in your coat pocket?"

The well- dressed man said quietly "it is meant to be. Soon you will be at a café called the Interlude Café. At the lower ground floor, a small green goblin will meet you.

James turned to speak to the stranger, but he was gone. In his hand was this expensive tailored blue over coat. He was in shock and could not tell what had just happened was real. He put the coat on and felt a warm sense of comfort and put his hands into the pockets. In one pocket was a photograph of all of them as kids with their mum.

Interlude Cafe

James just appeared at the Interlude Cafe.

He had no idea how he got there, but he was

still wearing the blue overcoat. He entered the

café and walked down the steps to the lower

ground floor. There was a lady with a hair net

on, in nineteen forties clothing.

"Hello love, is it James?

"Yes, but I'm confused. Where am I?

"You are at the Interlude Café and a man is

waiting for you at the bottom of the stairs."

He got to the bottom step and noticed a green

door at the back of the room. Standing near the

door was a small man with a Fez hat on.

The small man smiled, "Hello James, I have been expecting you. Can I see your voucher?"

James was still in shock, that the man knew his name. "How do you know my name?"

The small man ignored his question and repeated "can I see your voucher for Hamley's?

James handed the little man the voucher given by his brother.

The small man said "Thank you and opened the green door. We don't have much time, but urge you to enter please. I can't explain, all we be revealed."

James did as he was told. He left the voucher with the small man and entered the green door.

James found himself in a field with long grass, he was at the end of an army patrol. He could hear gun fire and felt really scared.

He buried his face into the mud. Someone tapped him on his back, in a reassuring voice "James, it's me Steven. You need to keep up and keep your wits about you."

James rubbed his eyes, it really was his brother. James followed the patrol and was mesmerised by Steven. Then the noise of gunfire and mortars, as they came under attack. Bullets whistled over James's head. Steven controlled the patrol as they hit the ground and returned fire. Then Steven noticed a woman with two children caught up in the cross fire. Steven told his men to cover him. James watched as his brother ran out to the woman and children. He shielded the woman and her two sons to safety. It was in this vulnerable position that he was killed by machine gun fire. James got up to run to his safety. The next thing he was with Steven in a nineteen forties cafe called The Interlude Cafe. It had the decor like the Second World War era.

A woman with a headscarf, showed the brothers to a table. She handed them a menu with the name on the front page, The Interlude Cafe. James had tears running down his face. Steven came over and hugged his beloved brother. "What's going on Steven?"

Steven did not let go, "this is the last time we will see each other until you die. The green door on the wall is a portal to the afterlife."

"I don't understand bruv, what do you mean? They all hugged together tightly and then their Mum entered.

"Mum where am I, are you real" said James. She smiled "this is real, there is a life after. Steven has joined me in this amazing and lovely place. We do not have much time James. I wanted to say how proud I am of you, Joanne and my wonderful grandson Steven. I have never stopped loving you both, you both turned out great people."

She poured a cup of tea for her boys. James sipped it and really felt the love of his mum. James smiled as tears of joy fell down his face. "That was the best cup of tea ever."

The next thing the man with the trilby appeared at the café's entrance. James hugged his mum and Steven. They all hugged and cried.

The man handed back the Hamley's voucher to James, "you may need this one day. Can I have my coat back?"

James handed the blue coat back to the man.

The small man with the fez appeared near a green door. James made his way to the man with the Fez and turned to the well-dressed man. "Thank you for this amazing rich spiritual experience. I am not sure if this is just a dream, but I am really thankful."

He walked through the green door and found himself back at Wimbledon Park.

Refugee

A war plane roared over the skies, the force of the planes rocked the village below. Then the skies seemed to quieten. There was an eerie silence, followed by a loud explosion. Imploding vacuum of glass and shrapnel impaled on women, children, elderly and adults.

Doctor Yusuf Omar was a Psychologist sitting at his home, having their evening meal as a family. The silence then followed by incredible loud explosion. He awoke bewildered covered in dust and rubble, blood was running down his head. He looked to see where his wife, daughter and son was.

He used his bloodied cut hands to remove the rubble and bricks. The smell of sulphur and smoke filled the area around Yusuf. With limited visibility he crawled across the rubble, feeling for his family. He finally could feel some clothing and started to claw through the rubble. His vision was prohibited by all the smoke, but under some bricks, was his wife Anita and their twelve year old daughter Ishia. They were both dead. Yusuf screamed out in pain and tears streamed down his face. He started to dig around his wife and daughter with his bare hands. He was shouting for his son "Asif, Asif can you hear me!" He could not see or feel for his son.

He kept shouting "Asif, Asif can you hear me.

Yusuf was traumatised and his whole body was in shock.

The war was destroying his people and country. Life was cheap and killing was part of every day.

After some time a local family came to help. Yusuf would not leave his family home. They took his wife and daughter on stretchers. He was frozen in shock and pain and kept digging for his son. Local community came to help and started to dig with Yusuf, to find Asif.

Six Months Later

Yusuf had escaped his war torn country. He was forty five years old, his wife, children and parents were brutally killed. His other teenage son was missing. He escaped being killed and suffering from trauma to get to Europe, first Germany and then settling in the United Kingdom. His former role was a Psychotherapist and Psychologist. But his qualifications were not suitable in the UK. He worked in a restaurant, in Wimbledon at night and cleaned a local school in the mornings. He missed his country and was still suffering from trauma from what happened to his family.

He had other relatives trapped in his country and worried for their lives. He had no way to contact his family.

He was desperate to get a job doing what he loved, helping people with social, emotional and mental health issues. He enrolled on a counselling course and thought this would help him gain employment as a therapist.

He shared a bedsit with five other families. Every night he could not sleep due to the horrors of the war. He kept seeing his family dead. Waking up in cold sweats screaming his son's name.

Yusuf was suffering from post- traumatic stress disorder, the trauma and loss had made him clinically depressed.

He felt such guilt for the loss of his family, his thoughts were invasive and the guilt of his loss, made him suicidal. He did not want to live any more.

Every day his body struggled with the weight of loss, guilt and no energy. It was like he was wearing one of those old diving bell suits with weights on your body and feet.

Yusuf would always bring food from the restaurant where he worked and give it to the families, where he was living.

He would go to the Syrian embassy in London every day, to see if they had found his son. Everyday no news sent him into deeper depression and he kept blaming himself for the loss of his whole family.

Winter

London was having a freezing spell of cold
weather. It had been snowing for several days
now. Yusuf could not afford a winter coat and
shivered all the way to work. On his way home
from his cleaning job, he decided to look into a
charity shop for a coat. The man working in
the charity shop was stylish and wore a trilby
hat. He asked Yusuf "are you looking for a
new coat? Because we have just received this
new coat for just five pounds. It is a gorgeous
blue camel wool coat."

Yusuf tried it on and it was a bit big, but it was
so warm. He put the coat on, it just had an
amazing feel of positivity.

He bought it for five pounds. "Thank you sir, this is a wonderful coat." He walked home wearing the coat.

Evening

That evening he got ready early for his work at
the restaurant, as he was going to visit a friend
who lived near Vauxhall Bridge. He got off the
tube station and started to walk to his friend's
flat. But for some reason he ended up at
Vauxhall Bridge. No matter what road or
direction he took, he ended up at the bridge.
The snow was still falling, the white and cold of
the heavy snow made the city an eerie stillness.
The next thing some people were shouting for
help. Yusuf ran over and a man said a young
person has just jumped off the bridge into the
water. Without hesitation, Yusuf went to help.
For some reason the coat would not come off.

He just jumped in from the path into the River
Thames. Some how he felt calm and buoyant
with the heavy coat on. He swam strongly
across the strong pull of the river's currents.
He saw the young person with his hands up in
the water, struggling for his breath. Yusuf
swam to the young person and as he got close
realised that it was son, Asif.

"Asif, my son. God be with us."

"Father, help me."

Yusuf held on to his son and swam on his side.
As he got near the bank a well-dressed man
threw a safety ring to Yusuf and pulled them in.

Yusuf was full of emotion and carried his son

from the bank, soaking wet in the snow,

freezing.

Yusuf screamed "help me, my son may die.

A man in the trilby appeared and helped Yusuf.

"Trust me, we are going to somewhere warm."

There was a flash of light, they were outside the

Interlude Café. There was sign in the window

which read treacle tart for one penny. As they

entered the café there was a lady with a hairnet

on, she was holding two blankets.

"You must be freezing gentleman, she put a

blanket around Asif and one around Yusuf.

She took them to a table. She made them her

special tea and her warming ginger nut biscuits.

Yusuf cried "son are you ok?

"Father, you saved me? I did not want to live any more, we lost all our family. I thought you were dead and I could not see the point of living."

"I felt the same my beautiful son, but God has brought us together."

The well-dressed man put his arm around Yusuf and his son. "Yusuf in the coat you are wearing, is a pocket with an envelope. Please get it out."

Yusuf reached inside the coat, which was unbelievable dry. He pulled an envelope out and opened it. It had a legal document and two sets of keys.

He read the document detailing that he fully owned the house in Balvernie Grove SW18.

"Excuse me sir, I think this information must belong to someone else.

"No Yusuf, this house is for you and your son to build your lives again. You deserve this."

"I don't understand, where am I? How can I afford a house?

"Yusuf, everything is paid and there is a special bank account to help you."

Soon I will have to go. Once I put on my coat, you will be outside your new home. Just open the door with your set of keys, all the paperwork is in the house. The house is fully furnished and there is food in the fridge."

Asif confused "Father, what's going on. Have we died?"

The well-dressed man looked at the lady in the café.

She said "no Asif, life has just started for you and your Father."

"Thank you Yusuf, you and your son are amazing, brave people. I am so sorry for your loss and pain."

The well-dressed man put on his coat and wiped the tears of sorrow from his eyes. He walked forward into a tunnel of bright light.

The Head

Jo Kiely has been appointed as the new Head Teacher at the worst school in the country. Head of Mayfield Secondary School, Wandsworth. The schools bad reputation, has made this school a notorious place of bad behaviour, failing results, drugs, crime, teenage pregnancies and violence. Most of its pupils are living in a disadvantaged London, living in tower blocks and estates where families struggle to keep their heads above the poverty line. For many of the pupils, school is the only place to get a hot meal and feel secure.

Jo spent her first six months getting to know the staff and pupils, to assess what strategies and plans were needed going forward. Her assessment showed that seventy per cent of the pupils were struggling to cope at school. There was a lot of pupils who struggled with their mental health, social and emotional issues. Because the majority of her pupils were struggling to cope at school and home, this put a lot of pressure on the teaching staff. Over one hundred pupils had been excluded to behavioural centres (Pupil Referral Units). She noted a lot of her pupils were smoking, or smoking marijuana in school.

There were several girls who were pregnant, drug dealers hanging outside school trying to groom pupils into their gang culture. Most of the pupils had low self- esteem, no motivation to achieve and a lack to better their lives. They have grown up with poverty, abuse, violence, drugs and alcohol dependency. These teenagers had been surrounded by negative language, being shouted at, nobody ever asked their opinions or praised them. The financial recession had increased their deprivation and poverty. Social classing was forcing families in London to other areas of the country, due to a lack of accommodation.

Crime became the quickest answer out of this black hole, for many families and young people. The foodbanks showed people queuing in their hundreds.

At school these labelled young people just got into more bad behaviour, their dysfunctional label was normal part of their lives. Being hard and a trouble maker gave them status and encouraged more riskier behaviour

No one had taken the time to find out about these young people, what their strengths were, what issues they were facing, how many families were living in poverty.

Some pupils who were now groomed in to gangs.

This meant they were carrying knives, sometimes guns to school. Two police officers and security staff were recruited at the main gates, to search all young people and their bags.

Jo presented a hundred page report for her CEO of the academy and senior leadership team.

Her CEO Lionel Jamesson was a notorious narcissist, who just wanted results. In his last role, he managed to get rid of many experienced staff. Staff who had committed many years to this school. He restructured and many people lost their jobs.

Lionel in his tailored blue suit just shrugged the report.

"This report is just a lot of excuses and hot air, he looked at the Senior Leadership Team. I am giving you six months Jo, to turn this failing school around."

Lionel Jamesson checked his mobile, "right apologies, I have to attend another meeting." He picked up his things and left. It was like a dark thunder cloud had just flown over them. To add to the problems there was a high turnover of staff. The school is mainly made up of supply staff. There was no continuity for the pupils. Parent's had also been violent and dangerous towards staff and other families. Pupils came from generations of problems and issues.

Jo's first task was to recruit permanent good teachers. She developed her own vision for the school, every child counts.

Jo actively lead from the front, she always welcomed children and parents in the playground before school. She developed a system to help her motivate her pupils, she called it STAR.

It stood for Strengths, Teamwork, Attitude and Rewards. She presented this first to her staff, detailing that shouting and screaming at pupils will result in disciplinary action.

"We need to understand our pupils, what their strengths are, what issues they have at home and school.

I want a new Special Education Needs Co-ordinator (SENCO) and pastoral team to support children who have social, emotional and mental health issues. I also want to run a project to help feed families. I have got many supermarkets to donate food which is close to the sell by dates. This will mean that we can help feed the child and their families.

Vision

Jo started her role by finding out about the pupils in her school. She wanted to establish why kids hated school? What was going on at home, what skills and talents each child has? She worked and motivated her teaching and support staff, using the slogan "Young people are our future to a better world."

She recruited a whole new team which included a pastoral team, incorporated many sports, arts and creativity, music clubs and after school activities. Every morning they did mindfulness, yoga classes.

She worked hard to make sure individuals were positively praised and rewarded for doing good things.

She never gave up on any pupil, she always gave each child a voice and someone to listen to. Pupils started achieving and were happy to come to school. She set up the "The Freedom to Write" club. This gave young people a platform to express themselves by writing poetry, Rap, diaries, journals and stories about their bravery of survival on the streets.

Jo would be working from six am to midnight, working hard to safeguard vulnerable children, tackle poverty by paying for uniforms, food and stationery for parents.

She paid out of her own money for parenting classes and helped with parent's education. She ran after school classes for pupils in all subjects.

Jo was too busy to be tackling negativity, she was dealing with issues where a mother and son had been severely beaten by her partner, that they became homeless on the streets of London. Children who had severe anxiety, on the autistic spectrum with no support, or a young person's parent who had been involved in a gang shooting. This was the only place a lot of the children could get a hot meal.

All other Government agencies were fully stretched and could not cope with the demands of families and young people who needed professional help. These agencies had been cut by austerity and lacked the professionals to support families and children.

Jo was making a difference, she now had great teachers and support staff. But the constant negativity from outside and the bullying from the CEO was starting to make her ill. She could feel that her mental health was suffering. She felt that her work was not enough. She had become severely depressed, but put on a brave face for her colleagues.

One afternoon Jo could see some of the drug dealers outside the school gate. They surrounded around one of the school pupils, he looked terrified.

She called the police, but due to cuts to their service, they could not promise a police person for hours.

She went through the main gate and asked her pupil Steven to come into school. He was so scared. The three drug dealers looked at Jo.

"You better get back into your warm school, bitch."

Jo ignored the comment, "Steven make the right decision now." Steven ran through the main gate.

The gang leader looked at Jo, "you are dead Steven, you and your family are in big trouble bro."

The gang leader walked over to Jo and put his face into her face, starring at her with violent eyes.

He went to punch her in the face. His punch was stopped in mid flow by a well-dressed man in a blue coat and wearing a trilby. The well-dressed man squeezed the gang leader's hand, breaking small bones. The gang leader screamed and fell to the ground crying in pain. He starred at the gang leader's eyes and then picked him up, like a piece of paper and threw him at the other two gang members.

It was like a bowling alley as the gang leader knocked the other two lads over. Their fall shocked them, as they realised that they were up against a force. They got up and ran up the road.

"Excuse me Mam, are you okay?"

She nodded but was trembling with fear. The well- dressed man put his blue coat over Jo's shoulders.

Then this bright light appeared and she found herself outside the Interlude Café with the well-dressed man. He opened the door for Jo, she walked in confused.

"Where am I?"

"I just thought you could do with a cup of tea?"

A lady with a hairnet and an apron arrived with a pot of tea and some home baked ginger biscuits. "There you go lovey. You are one brave Head Teacher, facing them no good wise guys."

"How did I get here, is this real?"

"We are here to help you Jo.

The well-dressed man said "What if I could take you to the future and show what happens to one of your pupils. We will see what happens with your great work and without your care?"

Jo looked up "who are you, how do you know I have pupils?

"Firstly do you mind if I call you Jo?

Jo said "no, but how do you know my name? I am a Head Teacher and want my kids to be happy and safe."

"I know Jo. This is not easy to comprehend or make any rational sense, but trust me. I am helping you see that your work makes a difference. We are going to the future 2030 and let's see what happens to one of your pupils without and with your help and support."

2030

Jo opened her eyes to find herself in
Wandsworth in 2030, there was a fast train on
overhead magnetic rails. She saw a greater
presence of police on the streets, they were all
armed.

The well-dressed man looked at Jo "now let's
see one of your pupils without your care first."
Jo found herself walking down Merton Road,
but this time there was a huge police presence,
as they put police tape around the crime scene.
She sees that they have arrested a man for
murder.

It was one of her pupils, Danny Stewart.

Then the well-dressed man appeared. "Now we walk down the same road, but the only difference is the care and support you gave to this young person."

Jo walked down Merton Road, there had been a road traffic accident near the Park Tavern Pub. An ambulance arrived with a paramedical team and a Doctor. The Doctor was Danny Stewart. The well-dressed man said "you will know this pupil as Danny Stewart. Danny has two choices one he joins a gang, as he felt he had no purpose. Getting into organised crime made him a target for other gangs and the police. Or you show him that someone believes in him, he is a clever lad, who will go on to be a doctor."

"I feel all the responsibility for Danny is all down to me."

"You will make a difference to so many children, teenager's lives. Don't worry about your CEO. He has a shock coming to them on Christmas Eve."

They appeared at the Interlude Café, in a tunnel of bright light.

"I can't believe what's just happened." She sipped her tea and tried a ginger biscuit. Her eyes lit up, she felt like she was hit with amazing light, it was so calming and reassuring.

The lady with the hair net and the apron, came to the table and seemed panicked, "it is time to go my love, German planes are just starting to bomb."

Jo opened her eyes and she was outside the school gates. She stood tall and walked calmly back into school.

Christmas Eve 2019

The CEO had been busy partying on Christmas Eve, all part of expenses. Knocking back the Prosecco and cocktails with his Directors. Recently divorced and left his wife and son. His son is now sixteen and has been struggling with his mental health and drug addiction. He ignores the text from his son, asking for help. When he got home at two AM, he fell into bed drunk and out of his mind. Clothes and money sprawled all over the bedroom floor. He got into bed with a lady he met that night. In the early hours of the night he was awoken by a high pitched sound and a smell of garlic.

As he awoke up in a drunken stupor, a man wearing a trilby was sat opposite.

"Who are you, I don't have any money."

"I am the ghost of Christmas and I am going to show you your future and the future of your children."

"Who are you?" He tried to get up and fell off the bed. He was overcome by the bright light. He opened his eyes to see he was walking with the well-dressed man walking down Smeaton Road.

There were some lads ahead up the street chatting, when a car drove past and opened fire. One of the lads fell to the floor in a pool of blood.

As the CEO got close he realised that he was his son. He fell to his knees and tried to revive his son. His son was holding onto his mobile phone.

They both died.

He looked at the well-dressed man, "please help me, what can I do to save him?"

"First, check your mobile phone messages."

The CEO broke down and cried. "He was asking for my help and I was too busy getting drunk."

"When we go back to your real world, you can start by cleaning your life up. This time is in the future, you will go back to a time where you can make a difference.

A difference to your son and to Jo Kiely and the amazing school she runs. By the way your Head Teacher is amazing, she will help a lot of young people. If you mess her around, you will have me to deal with."

Christmas Day

The CEO awoke, he got dressed and sent a text to Jo and all his staff wishing them "A Merry Christmas to my amazing staff."

He got in his car and drove to where his ex-wife and son lived. He brought them some presents and came to say sorry. He made peace with his ex-wife and his son.

In fact he remarried his ex-wife and became a mentor and friend to his son. His son went on to run their own building business and gave the CEO grandchildren. Also the CEO changed his behaviour and morals and made sure he looked after his amazing school staff and especially his talented Head Teacher Jo Kiely.

The Dad's Club

Antonio Raffella was a proud Dad of two sons.

He dedicated himself to his wife and family.

He worked hard as a brick layer and had lovely

times with his kids. He was a keen Chelsea

football fan and often took the family to see

premiership games. As the boys became

teenagers his older son Jamie who was fifteen

and wanted to go to the game with his school

mates. Antonio wanted Jamie to be happy and

have some independence and gave him

permission.

Antonio was working one Saturday and got a

call from his wife.

"Come home Antonio, Jamie has been stabbed and attacked. Please come home now, the doctor says he is critical."

As Antonio and his wife Sharon got to St. George's Hospital, they ran in and were met at reception by a Police woman and a doctor. They were ushered to a private room. The doctor sadly told them "Jamie had died due to his injuries. I can't tell you how sorry I am. We tried our best to revive Jamie, but his injuries were too severe."

Antonio and Sharon broke down and could not believe their child had died.

Antonio looked at the policewoman, "do you know who did this to my wonderful son?

"Mr Raffella, we are now investigating a murder enquiry. We will do everything we can to catch these animals."

"Why would some gutless person kill a harmless person, who has never had a fight? I vow I will get this person or people, I will get these people until I die."

The grieving for Jamie was immensely painful and difficult for all the family. He vowed revenge and he would get those who murdered his son. Antonio and the parents of Jamie's friends met regular for a drink. All the Dads were in agreement, enough is enough, and they had to take the law into their own hands.

Antonio set up the Dad's club and all the Dads were up for it. They felt Antonio's pain and revenge was the answer. The Dads club was a vigilante group that would drop everything if any of their family members was in trouble. The Dads made a pact, one for one and one for all. This often meant violence, against those who chose to pick upon vulnerable people. Drug gangs grooming school children as young as ten, the message would get back to the Dad's Club. Due to all the police cuts, they could only offer a limited service. Dad's had to take the law into their own hands.

This meant getting ready for any eventuality, arming with weapons and guns.

Antonio was not going to stop and wanted revenge for his son's killers.

A different type of violence was hitting the streets of Wandsworth. Drug gangs and bullies were thinking twice about their actions, as the crime rate started to lower. This had not happened in many years. It was a bit like the old East End days, scumbags who preyed on their own people, got dealt with. The Dad's club were anonymous and the police turned a blind eye to their actions. One drug gang leader was beaten and they put him in a cage high on a crane.

From the cage hanged a giant banner with his name on it and the crimes he has committed. He was finally released by the police and fire brigade.

While in custody, the slippery gang leader made a deal. He could not face going inside, as there were people who wanted him dead, for grassing previously. He told the Detective in the interview he knew the people who killed the Raffella boy. The drug gang leader was released on a witness protection scheme.

Word on the Street

Antonio via the Dad's Club, had many contacts
and some in the police. He had been giving
some information to the whereabouts of the
person who killed his son. The anger and
grieving the loss of his son was so deep and
painful, he could only think of revenge.

He was not good with his mental health and had
spent years trying to find the killers and bring
them to justice. Due to the fear these gang
members caused to the local residence, no one
would come forward. He knew their addresses
now and started to plan his attack. He did not
tell the other Dads, as he knew this would end
up in a blood bath.

Revenge

After several weeks of meticulous planning, he knew who he would target first. It was Wednesday twenty first of November 2019 at two am. Armed with a hand gun, an automatic weapon and several grenades. He got in his car and drove up Wimbledon Park Road for the turn off for Augustus Road. It was early morning, his eyes were adjusting to the darkness and he was full of fear and adrenalin. He opened his car window to let the cool air in. He must have taken his eye of the road for a second. He heard a bang and saw a man with a hat lying in the road. He stopped the car just before Southfields Station and got out the car.

He carefully went over to the man, who was wearing a trilby hat and a coat. He touched the man on his back feeling the damp of the coat material. Then instantly from the touch, there was an explosion of light.

Antonio then opened his eyes and found he was standing with a well- dressed man outside a café called The Interlude. The well-dressed man opened the door to the café and said "you could do with a coffee."

Antonio was confused "where am I? Are you okay, my car must have hit you?"

"Please come in with me."

So Antonio entered the café. The café was all old fashioned, nineteen forties style.

A lady with a big beaming smile, a hairnet and one of those aprons grandmothers used to have. She let Antonio sit down and bought two slice of his favourite cake, Panetone. Also a strong coffee and a lemonade drink.

The well-dressed man looked at the café owner and thanked her. "I know this may seem crazy, but someone special is here to see you. Please, please you must listen."

From the green door at the end of the café, a teenage boy came out and sat with Antonio. It was his son who had been killed.

Antonio grabbed his son and held him tight, tears flooded Antonio and his son Jamie.

Jamie looked at his Dad, "Dad I know you want revenge. But violence and murder is not the way. You will end up in prison for murder. Mum and all the family would have to go through even further pain."

"Jamie my beautiful son, I can't let these scum bags get away with it. They will do it again to someone else."

"Dad I am begging you, I don't have long to speak. I promise you that they will get their justice."

The well-dressed man took off his coat and walked over to Antonio and his son.

He was holding Antonio's holdall with all his weapons. "Can I have your hand gun please Antonio?"

Jamie held his Dad, "please Dad.

Antonio handed it over to the well-dressed man.

He handed the bag to the owner of the café.

The well-dressed man thanked Antonio. "They will get their justice, believe me. I am sorry but Jamie will have to go back."

"Love you Dad, tell Mum and everyone I am okay and will see you all one day. Don't be sad Dad, life is good on this side. It's time for you to start to live again."

Antonio then found himself near to his car, he had a puncture in both front tyres.

He decided to leave the car and walk home to his beautiful wife. He was so overwhelmed with the happiness he got from meeting Jamie. He walked down Wimbledon Park Road, when he saw the Well-dressed man.

"Hi Antonio, I forgot to give you this. He reached inside the coat and it was Jamie's football badge. "Jamie said he wanted you to have this and will always be around you and your wife."

Antonio took Jamie's badge. "Thank you, you must be a guardian angel."

The well-dressed man tipped his trilby with his hand and walked up the road.

Later that day local news said "that four men died in a car accident, after being pursued by the police. They believe one of the four men was wanted for the murder of Jamie Raffella."

The Jobs On

Charlie Ainsworth an ex retired bank robber, he served in the Special Forces in his youth.

Charlie could not settle when he came out of the forces. He decided to put his knowledge of explosives and specialist training, breaking into the rich and elite safes and deposit boxes.

Over the years Charlie had been given the nick name "Charlie Hood" as most of the money he stole ended up into charities, he never benefitted from the stash. It was just for the thrills.

In and out of prison had taken its toll on Charlie and he decided to retire and hang up his boots.

Recently he had just found out that he has final stage cancer and weeks or months to live. When Charlie came out of the forces, his girlfriend at the time gave birth to a daughter. But because of his life style and not being able to settle, he lost touch with her. He always thought of her and carried the pain in his heart. He began to look for his daughter, time was not on his side. But wanted to do one more job. Some inheritance for his daughter and her family, if she has one.

The Last Job

Charlie knew all the old crew had passed away,
many of them died in prison. He had promised
his mates that he would look after their spouses
and their kids who were struggling financially.
He had kept to his word.

But now there was nothing to lose and this time
he wanted to use technology to hack into off
shore bank accounts. The money he retrieved
would not be traced as those who deposited it,
did so illegally.

One day he heard a knock on his flat door. He
went to the door and standing there was this
well-dressed man, with a trilby hat and a blue
overcoat.

"Can I help you mate?"

"Yeah, I am looking for Charlie Hood?

"Who is asking?"

"Easy Charlie, we did some time together and I
need a place to lay low for a while."

Charlie never turned his back on his own kind
and invited the man in.

What do they call you?

"Alfred Cap, my nick name was scar face."

"Well my memory is not as good these days.

What prison was it?

"It was Wandsworth, a long time ago."

No, problem pal, you are welcome here. Are
the old bill after you?"

Not at the moment, but they will be."

"What do you mean?

"I want to do a last job. I am not getting

younger and I want one last adventure."

Charlie smiled "What do you have in mind?

Both men started laughing.

The man took off his trilby and said "I can hack

into offshore bank accounts without a trace."

"What, no way!"

"Watch me Charlie Boy."

Alfred got a lap top from his coat and logged

in.

Charlie looked confused "that's some coat.

What else have you got in there?"

Alfred laughed, "The coat is magical, and it has

everything you need."

Over the next weeks Charlie had managed to steal millions and bank it all in a separate Swiss bank accounts. His health had deteriorated and he was on his last days on Earth. He also managed to transfer money to the Grenville Tower charity and to help his former colleague's families. Before his last breaths, he looked at Alfred.

"Make sure my daughter gets the money." His breathing laboured and stoked like an old boiler, he died as Alfred held his hand.

Alfred cried and said a pray, "sometimes life throws you difficult obstacles, they might have called Charlie a criminal, but his heart was that of a good man.

I have never understood why the wealthy and

powerful can constantly steal, lie and cheat, but

get away with it?"

Single Mum

Kim was twenty years old and living in a run-down bed sit, with her two year old daughter. She was a single parent. Her mum had become an alcoholic and lived on the streets. Her dad had never been on the scene, since she was six. He ended up in prison and we lost touch. Mum Kathy could not cope and alcohol became her release. Kathy's circulation had been impaired by the alcohol and she developed chronic leg ulcers and eventually died of septicaemia. Kim received benefits that barely covered the bills and food. Often Kim went without food and every penny went on her daughter.

Living in poverty was having its toll on her mental health, she dreaded the post. Every day she did her best to make meals and spend quality time playing with her bundle of joy. Her saviour through this harsh reality was her pen and makeshift notebook. Kim had a talent for writing and loved to write stories. But due to her financial situation, she had to utilise people's scrap rubbish paper for her notebook. She loved to put her imagination onto paper. Each month revealed the bare cupboards and the darkness of survival. Taking the pens from betting shops, to support her only freedom, to escape in a world of fantasy.

She was nearing the end of her children's book. It was about a single parent whose son gets to go with his Uncle, who was a space pirate, protecting planet Earth. One day an alien race called the Hungalians comes and kidnaps Father Christmas and tries to stop Christmas on Earth.

Kim was hit with deep depression. No one wanted to help her or listen to her. Her past of her mum and not seeing her dad haunted her. The guilt and loss had severely affected her. Every time she phoned for medical help, they would tell her to phone First Response. She would phone and no one could help her.

Kim was at an all-time low, no one cared. She was just given medication. She became desperate and started thinking there was no point to living?

Kim got a friend to look after her daughter, she was at an all- time low. She wanted to go for a walk, to clear the fog in her head. She took the canal path through Wandsworth, walking down the River Wandle, when all of sudden she lost her footing and stumbled into the canal. She was struggling some weeds had wrapped around her legs. She kept going under. A well-dressed man dived in and saved her. He put his blue coat around Kim. Then she felt the heat from a bright light.

The Interlude Cafe

She was sitting in a nineteen forties café, a lady with a hairnet came over and brought a pot of tea over, with some home-made ginger biscuits. The lady poured the tea and calmly said "its ok lovey, my tea will warm you up."

The well-dressed man reassured Kim, "You are save. I know things have been really difficult for you. You are a brilliant Mum and you are going to be a famous author. Take a look at your inside pocket in the coat."

She reached in and pulled a paper copy of her book out. The title was The Adventures of Danny and Uncle Phil the Space Pirate by Kim Ainsworth.

"Where am I, is this some sort of I'm dead, is this the afterlife?"

"No, this is about second chances and not to give up on life and your dreams. Check your other inside pocket, this publisher has just sent you a letter of acceptance. You are going to be a famous author. But before you go back, someone wants to see you."

A green door opened from the back of the café and a man entered into the café.

"My darling daughter, it's me your old man. I am so sorry my darling for being a terrible Dad. Unfortunately, I have passed to the other side. I don't have long, but this great man Alfred helped me to find you.

I will get Alfred to put your inheritance into your account. You are going to be financially sound. I can't tell you that I have been thinking of you, all my life. I have had a pain in my heart. It was hard for your Mum and I take full blame." Charlie cried and hugged his daughter.

Kim shocked and not sure what to do next. Hugged her Dad and cried. "Seeing you Dad has been the best thing ever, I just wanted to hear that you loved me."

"I have always loved you. I have not got a lot of time, but this amazing man here will sort things out. I have to go my lovely girl, remember I am always by your side.

Go and make us proud with your amazing imagination and books.

Daughter and Dad hugged, while Alfred made the transfer of funds.

The bright light appeared and appeared with the well-dressed man outside a house in Balvernie Grove London. He handed her the keys and documents. Also he showed her the inherited funds, which was in a Swiss bank account.

Kim passed the coat back to the well-dressed man. Alfred reached in side one of the pockets and handed over a letter. She opened it and it was a publisher wanting to publish her children's book and offer a contract.

The well-dressed man smiled with happiness.

"Kim bring your daughter to your new home, you deserve this. You are a strong, brave woman and mum that will change her life and daughter's life."

The Interlude Cafe

The well-dressed man entered the Interlude Café. The owner of the café advised "that the Germans were planning heavy bombing raids tonight.

It's time Alphonse Gabriel Capone to hand your coat in. You have redeemed your past. What have you learned?"

Before I hand my coat on, I know now why I used my criminality to become rich. You see Italians in America in my time were treated worse than rats. I watched my parents struggle with the poverty and discrimination. Italians formed gangs, as we were vulnerable people.

I suppose poverty and seeing my family struggle, changed my life. Why couldn't I have, what the rich had? During the prohibition the rich elite were doing what we were doing. They did not go to jail, they got jobs in high powerful places. Yet I and others were criminals.

But this experience has been so emotional and difficult to see people in low and dark places. I now realise the importance of helping your family and helping people, showing care and understanding is what makes us human. All the material stuff is just false lies.

When you are at these dark times, you just need people to listen and care. With a bit of support you can help them back on track.

But charity and spirituality starts first at home with your own family. If I had my time again, my religion would be my family.

I am sorry for all that I have done in the past. If I had my time again I would live an ordinary life, wife and kids.

I know on this mission I broke your rules, in the way I helped some of the people. Like Charlie. But I just wanted to help, in the way I knew best. I also learned that we have not learnt our lesson about war and the effects it has on the human race.

If I could go back I would be a more peaceful person. This angel experience helped people who had lost their way. I just helped them get back on the track of life. "

"Thank you Alphonso, here is your expresso before you enter the green door. Your coat will be burnt. Each new angel gets a new tailored coat, made by myself. Thank you for making a difference to the people you helped back on their way."

"Ciao, signora."

Al Capone goes through the green door in the wall and is greeted by Mr. Fez, the small man takes him to where his family awaits him.